Based on the Marvel comic book series Spider-Man
Adapted by Clarissa S. Wong
Illustrated by Todd Nauck and Hi-Fi Design

Published by Marvel Press, an
imprint of Disney Book Group.
No part of this book may be
reproduced or transmitted in
any form or by any means,
electronic or mechanical, including
photocopying, recording, or by any
information storage and retrieval
system, without written permission
from the publisher.

For information address Marvel
Press, 114 Fifth Avenue, New York,
New York 10011-5690.
Printed in the United States of
America
First Edition
3 5 7 9 10 8 6 4 2
G658-7729-4-12156
ISBN 978-1-4231-5423-5

TM & © 2012 Marvel & Subs.

marvelkids.com

New York

One night, two boys went exploring in the Florida Everglades. They saw something sinister hiding in the swamp. "What is that?" one boy asked.

"It doesn't matter, let's get out of here!" his friend shouted.

Before long, the news reached New York and **Peter Parker,** an *almost* average Midtown High School student. The newspaper said the beast was almost seven feet tall with sharp teeth! They called it **the Lizard.**

J. Jonah Jameson, Peter's boss at *The Daily Bugle*, would pay a fortune for a photo of the Lizard! Peter needed the extra cash for Aunt May's birthday gift.

"What if I can get a photo of the Lizard **fighting Spider-Man?**" Peter asked. Jameson agreed, and now Peter would have to get an amazing shot of the Lizard. . .

. . . as Spider-Man! He heard the Lizard was spotted in the swamps. "I don't like it here at all. It's too quiet . . . and creepy." He wondered if the people who lived in the nearby house would know where the **swamps' latest celebrity** was hiding.

"Have you seen the Lizard?" Spider-Man asked.
The woman nodded with a sniffle. "You should leave.
The Lizard is my husband, **Dr. Curtis Connors!**"

"What?!" Spider-Man was so stunned
by the news that he almost fell off the roof!
He had heard of Dr. Connors before.

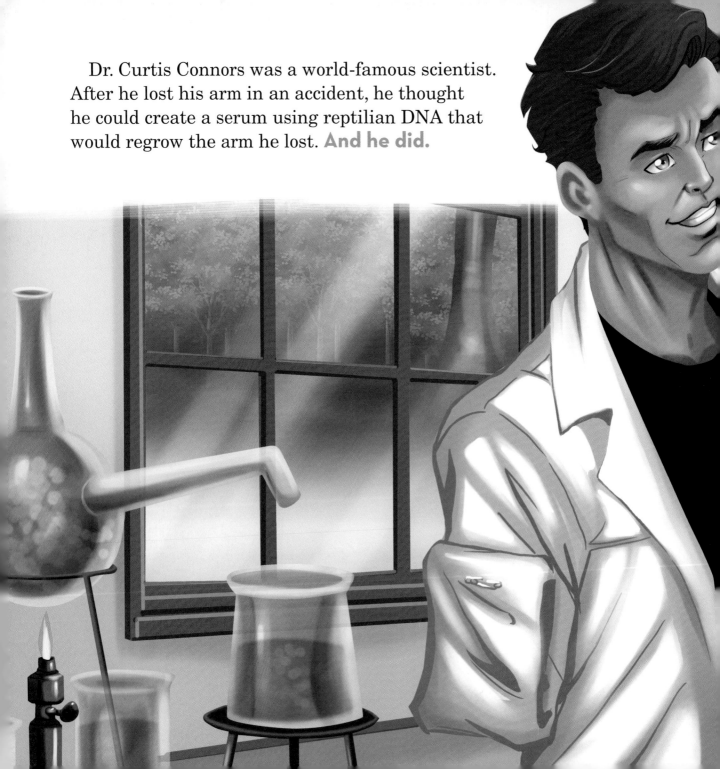

Dr. Curtis Connors was a world-famous scientist. After he lost his arm in an accident, he thought he could create a serum using reptilian DNA that would regrow the arm he lost. **And he did.**

Dr. Connors not only grew a new arm, but also scales, sharp claws, a tail, and a long, slimy tongue! He had transformed into **the Lizard.**

Every passing minute, he became less like Dr. Connors and more like a cold-blooded reptile. He did not want to scare his son, Billy, or his wife.

"I have to help the doctor, before it's too late..."
Spider-Man said. He studied Dr. Connors's notes.
"Are you a scientist, too, Spider-Man?" Billy asked.
"We'll find out soon enough!" Spider-Man said under
his breath as he worked.

Just then, Billy yelled, "Spider-Man, look!"

The lab door flew open. **It was the Lizard!** There were snakes and an army of reptiles with him! "What are you doing with my family?" the Lizard demanded.

"Trying to save you, Doc!" Spider-Man replied. The reptiles attacked Spidey, as if the Lizard was telling the reptiles what to do! Spider-Man tried to use his webbing. But, with one mighty swing of his tail, **the Lizard stopped Spider-Man's attack!**

The Lizard picked up a desk. "He's stronger than I had guessed!" Spider-Man ducked, barely escaping.

The web-slinger tried to fight back. **The reptile's skin was as hard as armor!** It almost broke Spidey's hand! "How pitiful!" The Lizard laughed.

The bigger snakes started to wrap around Spider-Man's limbs, holding him tight.

"Now, it's time to finish you off!" the Lizard growled.

Spider-Man knew this was his last chance! Quickly, he opened the test tube and poured the antidote into the Lizard's mouth. "Open wide, big guy!"

It was working! The other reptiles began to slither back to the swamp. "Say cheese, Doc!" Spider-Man said as he snapped a quick photo of his foe, just before he transformed back into Dr. Connors!

"I-I'm human again!" Dr. Connors shouted.

"Dad!" Billy rushed toward his father.

"Oh, Curtis, I can't believe you're really back!" Mrs. Connors hugged her husband.

The doctor thanked the spectacular Spider-Man, "Thank you for this priceless gift. **We'll never forget you!**"

Back in New York, Peter showed Jameson his photo of the Lizard. Jameson thought it was too good to be true.

"Where's Spider-Man? Why didn't you get a picture of the **Lizard and Spider-Man?**"

Jameson ripped up the photo. "This is a fake! I know it when I see it!"

Peter sighed.

Peter arrived at Aunt May's birthday party but without a special birthday gift.

"I wish I could have given you something really nice today," Peter said.

"But having you here is all I wanted!" She hugged him tightly.

Peter realized what was really important. Spider-Man had saved Dr. Connors, and he was still able to make it home in time for Aunt May's birthday. It was all part of being **the friendly neighborhood Spider-Man.**